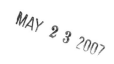

Verdi School Library
250 Bridge Street
Verdi, NV 89439

This book is dedicated to our husbands, Stewart Wilson and Bob Zerga,

for their support of our dreams

and for their concern for the animals in our woods.

The photographs in the story were not staged or altered.

We thank the real-life cowboys, Chad Alexander and John McDermitt,

who came to the rescue of the unfortunate deer.

ISBN: 0-9722570-1-2

Published by

Snowbound
BOOKS®

www.deertales.com

Book design by Julie Melton, The Right Type Graphics (USA)

Printed in Hong Kong

2004

Autumn Rescue

By Karen Collett Wilson

Photography by Susan A. Zerga

Did I ever tell you the story about the daring rescue that took place in our Cottonwoods not long ago? Gather near, and I'll tell you what happened.

It all began on a lazy autumn afternoon. The animals of the Cottonwoods were enjoying the last of Indian summer. (That is the time of warm summer-like days after the first nipping frost of autumn.)

The wild turkeys scratched the ground for grain and seeds while the migrating birds were gathering for their long flight south.

The nocturnal animals, the raccoons, skunks and porcupines, dozed in their sun-warmed, hollow tree trunks and burrows.

Even the royalty of the woods, the stately, graceful deer, were enjoying the perfect day. They browsed on rose hips and delicate tree shoots while serenely surveying their domain. All of the deer except one, that is.

One deer was too busy thinking about himself to notice anything else. He was thinking about his powerful legs, his luxurious coat, his noble nose and his superior ears. But, most of all, he was thinking about his exceptional antlers. They were large and wide and had many prongs.

He was so proud of his antlers that he polished them on tree branches ...

... and looked at their reflection in the pools of the languid creek. He was quite certain that his crown of antlers was the most royal of all.

It was then that the deer discovered something quite amazing.

While looking down to admire his hooves, the deer
saw a discarded circle of golden cord. It looked just like
a real crown, and he thought it would be perfect to adorn
his elegant antlers. He eagerly dipped his head and slipped
the golden coil in place.

But the decoration that had seemed so perfect soon became a problem. The cord drooped over his eyes, making it hard for the deer to see. It caught on low-hanging branches, making it difficult for him to walk through the woods. He even had trouble browsing on his favorite shrubs because the cord would tangle in them.

It was not long before the deer realized that he had made a terrible mistake. Instead of looking more beautiful, he knew that he looked foolish and not at all royal.

He decided it was time to remove the strange crown. He tried tipping and shaking his head, but the coil was stuck fast.

His deer friends looked at him with sympathy.

They tried, but they were unable to rid him
of his silly finery.

Days went by before the kind cowboys rode into the Cottonwoods. They saw at once that the unfortunate deer needed rescuing. (When cowboys brand or doctor their livestock, they must first lasso, or rope, them. The animals are then secure and will not hurt themselves or the cowboys.) The cowboys knew they would have to lasso the deer in order to untangle him.

So, very cautiously and very slowly, they moved toward the unhappy deer. When they were close enough, one of the cowboys skillfully threw his looped rope and lassoed one of the antlers.

Another of the cowboys expertly lassoed the other antler.

Then they carefully snubbed, or tied, the deer to a nearby tree for added protection from the sharp prongs. At last, the cowboys were able to remove the bothersome yellow cord.

The relieved and thankful deer was set free, and he returned safely to his herd.

That autumn afternoon slowly turned into evening.
The setting sun cast a golden glow over the land.

Another day had passed in the Cottonwoods. It might have been like so many others, except on that day a very haughty deer had finally been rescued.

Also by Karen Collett Wilson

and

Susan A. Zerga

Pogonip Magic